Find the Mistakes
Science Adventures

Remarkable Reptiles

Written by Julie Koerner
Illustrated by Greg Battes

Reviewed and endorsed by:
Harvey Fischer
Curator of Reptiles
Los Angeles Zoo

Copyright ©1990 by RGA Publishing Group, Inc.
Published by Price Stern Sloan, Inc.
360 North La Cienega Blvd., Los Angeles, CA 90048

ISBN: 0-8431-2809-7

10 9 8 7 6 5 4 3 2 1

PRICE STERN SLOAN, INC.
Los Angeles

Alligator

Have you ever heard of crocodilians? Even if the name doesn't sound familiar, you probably have heard of them, because all alligators and crocodiles are crocodilians.

You can tell alligators and crocodiles apart in several ways. Adult alligators are darker, almost black, and young alligators have yellow markings that crocodiles don't have. An alligator's snout is rounder and wider than a crocodile's pointed snout. And alligators have many more teeth, but who would dare to count them?

There are only two kinds of alligators in the world, and they are very much alike. The alligators once lived on the same land mass millions of years ago, but because the continents drifted apart, they now live on opposite sides of the world. The Chinese alligator, as you might guess, lives in China. The American alligator lives in the swamps, lakes and slow-moving rivers of the southeastern United States.

Alligators have some unusual eating habits. They eat fish, birds, small animals and even other reptiles. Maybe that doesn't sound so unusual for a reptile that grows almost 20 feet long, but did you know that they also swallow rocks? Alligators use their teeth for gripping and tearing, not for chewing their food. Some scientists think that the rocks help the alligators to grind their food.

Can you find and color 16 mistakes?

Crocodile

Scientists believe that alligators and crocodiles are the closest relatives we have to the extinct dinosaurs. In fact, ancestors of the modern crocodile did live during the dinosaur age, but they were much larger. One ancient crocodile was over 50 feet long, with long rear legs and short front legs. Sounds like a dinosaur, doesn't it?

Today, American crocodiles are found in the Florida Everglades, on some Caribbean islands, on the east coast of Central America and in the countries of Columbia and Ecuador. Lurking in the shallow water, they are often mistaken for logs because they have dark, bumpy skin, and they lie perfectly still.

As mentioned earlier, one good way to tell crocodiles apart from alligators is by their coloring. American crocodiles are gray with black markings, and alligators are nearly black. As both alligators and crocodiles get older, however, their colors fade and blend together. The best way to tell a crocodile from an alligator is to look at the teeth. When its mouth is closed, the crocodile's fourth bottom tooth on each side sticks out and shows very clearly. (These two teeth are much larger than the rest.) The alligator's fourth bottom teeth do not show unless the animal's mouth is open. So if you see these teeth, and the animal's mouth is closed, you can be certain you're looking at a crocodile!

Can you find and color 14 mistakes?

Gharial

You have learned that an alligator's snout is wide and rounded, and that the crocodile's snout is longer and more pointed. Another crocodilian has a snout that is the longest and most pointed of them all. The gharial (GAR-ee-ul), sometimes called the gavial (GAY-vee-ul), lives only in or near India. Its long, slender snout has a bump on the tip, and it's so long that it has been nicknamed "broom handle" or "frying pan handle." The gharial uses this snout to snare the fish it eats. Lying still at the bottom of a jungle swamp or stream, the gharial waits. When some fish approach, snap! The gharial traps a mouthful of fish.

We know that all crocodilians swallow hard objects such as stones, probably to help them digest their food. But did you know that gharials have also been known to swallow valuable necklaces, rings and other jewelry? Although gharials will not attack humans, they have been known to feed on dead bodies thrown into rivers after funeral services. Perhaps that's how the gharials swallowed the jewelry!

Can you find and color 14 mistakes?

Rattlesnake

If you're walking in the desert and suddenly hear a rattling sound break the silence, watch out—it may be a rattlesnake. Rattlesnakes are venomous pit vipers. Vipers have fangs that fold up when the jaw is closed and spring open when the jaw opens. When the snake bites, the fangs inject venom into the reptile's prey or attacker. Special heat-sensing organs, called pits, are located at the side of the viper's head. These organs tell the viper if the temperature near it changes even one degree. This helps it find and catch prey.

In North America, there are many kinds, or species, of rattlesnakes. Many have names that describe their color patterns, such as the diamondback rattlesnake or the banded rock rattlesnake. They live among the rocks and brush of the desert, and they occasionally climb trees. All rattlesnakes have one thing in common: the rattle at the end of their tail. When a rattlesnake is born, this rattle is a tiny button. Each time the snake sheds its skin as it grows, another segment is added to its rattle. By the time the snake is fully grown, it has an impressive rattle. When the snake feels threatened—usually by larger animals, such as a deer or bison—its tail makes a true rattling sound. Some people think the rattling sound means the snake is about to strike. Other people think the snake is saying "Don't step on me!" Whichever meaning is correct, we do know that sound means danger.

Can you find and color 14 mistakes?

8

Boa Constrictor

Have you ever seen the long feathery scarves that ladies sometimes wrap around their necks? That piece of fancy clothing—the feather boa—might be named after a snake, the boa constrictor.

Many snakes are constrictors. A constrictor kills its food by wrapping its strong body around its prey and squeezing until the prey stops breathing, or suffocates. After the animal has died, the boa constrictor swallows it whole! The boa eats animals such as small mammals, birds and occasionally lizards. The boa can detect the smell of its prey. It finds a place where it knows its prey visits and lies in wait. When the prey passes by, the boa strikes.

The powerful boa constrictor is considered one of the giants of the snake world; it grows to be 10 or more feet long. Its skin is dark reddish-brown with patterns (sometimes called "saddles") of lighter brown or grey on its back. The bright tail is marked with black dots and the underside is yellowish, also with black dots. One of the South American boa constrictors can grow even longer than 10 feet and has a dark coloring. Another South American boa, the emerald tree boa, is bright green, and it camouflages itself among the leaves of jungle trees, waiting for prey to come within its grasp.

Can you find and color 13 mistakes?

10

African Puff Adder

A very deadly snake that lives only in the African grasslands is the puff adder. Like the rattlesnake, this viper has long front teeth, or fangs, that inject venom into its prey when it bites. But unlike the rattlesnake, the puff adder doesn't have heat-sensing pits to help it find and catch prey.

About four feet long, the puff adder is gray or brown with white or yellow speckles. A pattern of wide, V-shaped black markings flows down its back, forming bands near the tail. Around each marking is a light yellow outline. These colors and pattern make for perfect camouflage in the adder's grassland home.

Like many other vipers, this snake has a thick body and a big, broad, flat head. All day long, the adder lies still, keeping cool from the sun in the sand or grass. At night, it lies in wait for rats, mice and birds to eat. When it spots its prey, it strikes with its venomous fangs.

Can you guess why this snake has such an unusual name? When it is threatened, the puff adder faces its enemy, takes in a deep breath to puff up its body, then lets the breath out with a long, hissing sound. That is why it's called the "puff" adder.

Can you find and color 13 mistakes?

Cobra

Cobras are known as the "snake charmer's snake." But the snake charmer's music-and-dance act isn't exactly what it appears to be. For one thing, that venomous snake isn't dancing—it's preparing to strike! When it feels threatened, the cobra holds its head up high and spreads its neck out flat and wide. This is called "hooding." The snake charmer plays his flute, and the snake appears to dance. But snakes can't hear! The cobra is only following the movement of the snake charmer's flute, staying alert to danger.

There are many different kinds of cobras. They all belong to a snake family called elapidae (eh-LAP-ih-day). Elapids have short fangs at the front of their mouths that inject venom into their prey when they bite. The king cobra of India is the largest venomous snake in the world. When threatened, the king cobra can raise half its body off the ground. A 12-foot-long cobra could raise 6 feet of its body off the ground and look a full-grown man in the eye! The female king cobra builds a nest of two chambers. She lays her eggs in the lower chamber, then sits in the upper chamber to keep watch.

The spectacled cobra, also from Asia, has a beautiful black-and-white design on the back of its head. Some African cobras can actually spit venom at their enemies' eyes. That's because the openings in their fangs are directed forward, rather than downward as in other venomous snakes.

Can you find and color 14 mistakes?

Hognose Snake

The hognose snake is a great actor! Although it is harmless, it acts like a very deadly snake when it is threatened. A frightened hognose puffs up its body, flattens its head and neck and makes a long hissing sound, just like the venomous puff adder does. If this act doesn't work, the hognose snake goes into Act II. It rolls over on its back, squirms and wiggles its body in the dirt, then collapses as though it were dead. It stays that way until it thinks the coast is clear. Then the snake slowly lifts its head to get a peek at the situation. If its enemy is still near, the hognose flops back down and plays dead again.

The hognose snake is so good at its act that people often mistake it for a viper. The truth is that it will never bite, except to catch food. Instead, this North American snake uses its turned-up snout to dig for its favorite food—toads. When the hognose snake finds a toad meal, it bites and swallows. Contrary to what some people think, the hognose snake does not make a good pet. The reptile needs so many toads to eat that it's hard to keep up with its appetite, and the creature usually starves to death.

Can you find and color 16 mistakes?

<u>Anaconda</u>

The largest snake in the world lives in the tropical rain forests of Central America. It is the anaconda, sometimes called the water boa because it spends most of its time in the water. Even though it is an excellent swimmer, the anaconda usually waits silently, with only its head sticking out of the water. It waits for small animals to come for a drink. An anaconda will eat any animal it can overpower, including birds, mammals, other reptiles and even turtles and caiman (another type of crocodilian). Like the boa, the anaconda is a constrictor. It kills its food by squeezing it to death.

This snake is huge! A large anaconda can grow to be over 20 feet long and more than 15 inches wide in the middle. The record for an anaconda is $37^1/_2$ feet. Imagine how wide that creature must have been!

Two rows of large round or oval spots cover the anaconda's olive-green body. On its sides are smaller spots against a yellowish-green background. Besides being larger than pythons, anacondas are different in another way: Pythons are hatched from eggs, but anacondas (and boas, too) are born live. At birth, an anaconda is already 30 inches long!

Can you find and color 14 mistakes?

18

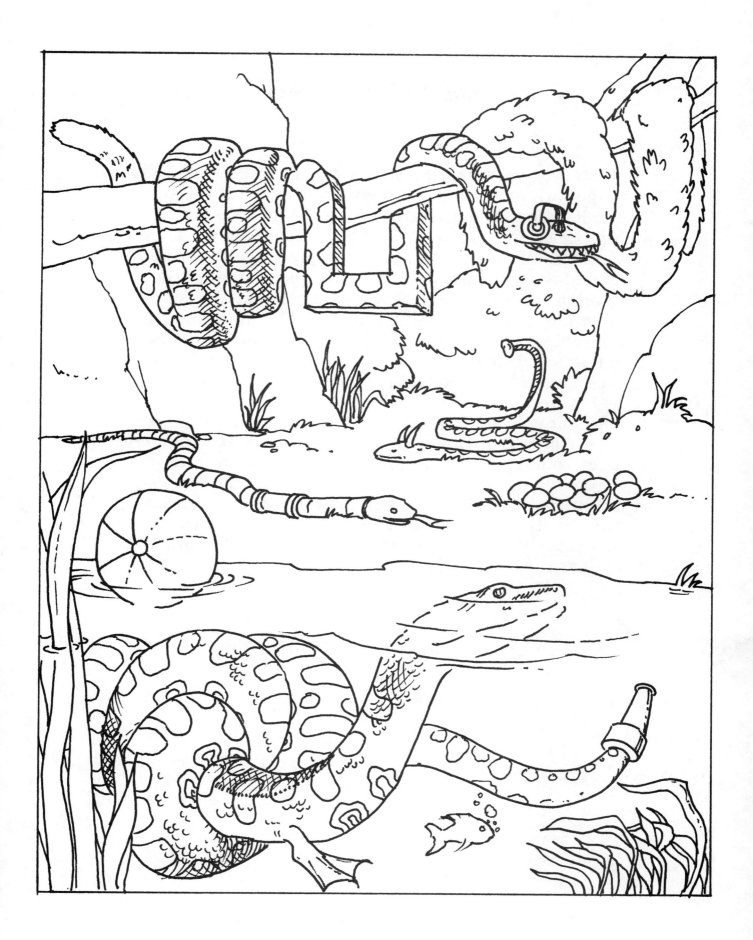

Fence Lizard

If you ever see a lizard near your home or in your neighborhood, it is most likely a fence lizard. These small, insect-eating lizards are found in parks, woods, lumberyards, empty lots and even playgrounds. There are more than 25 different kinds of fence lizards in the United States. Named "fence" lizards because of their habit of sunning themselves on fences, the reptiles can be tan, brown, green, gray or black. The underbelly of the males of some species is blue, so it won't surprise you to learn that some fence lizards have been nicknamed "blue belly."

Another common name for the fence lizard is the swift. The reason is obvious: These lizards move very quickly. They scurry up trees, rustle through leaves or scamper across a path. If a swift's tail is caught in an enemy's grasp, an amazing thing happens: The tail breaks off and the lizard runs away without it! A new tail will grow to replace the old one, although it will never be quite as long as the original tail.

Can you find and color 12 mistakes?

Chuckwalla

Long ago, the Indians gave a large desert lizard the name chuckwalla. Some species of this 18-inch lizard are dark brown or black. The males of other species have reddish-orange blotches on their backs and bellies. Whatever their color, the skin of the chuckwalla hangs loosely over the lizard's body. Yellow and black bands circle its tail. Like most desert lizards, the chuckwalla heats its body in the sun and keeps cool by lying between rocks. During the hottest part of the summer, it will burrow under rock or deep into rock crevices to escape the heat.

Even though the chuckwalla looks totally relaxed as it rests on a hot desert rock, it is almost impossible to surprise it. That's because it has very sharp eyesight. This keen eyesight allows the chuckwalla to see when danger is near. Its eyesight (and sense of smell, too) also helps the chuckwalla to find food. This desert lizard eats leaves, grasses, flowers and fruits.

The chuckwalla has a unique way of protecting itself from its enemies. First, it hides in a crevice between rocks. Then, it breathes air into its lungs in one big gulp. Its inflated body becomes wedged so tightly into the small space that the enemy cannot pull it out!

Can you find and color 14 mistakes?

22

Komodo Dragon

If you want to get an idea of how big a small dinosaur was, go to the tiny island of Komodo in Indonesia. There you'll find the Komodo dragon, a huge lizard that can be over 10 feet long and weigh up to 300 pounds. The fearsome-looking creature has loose, brownish-yellow skin that is covered with scales that look like tiny pebbles. Don't be surprised if you hear this "dragon" called the Komodo monitor, because the reptile actually belongs to a family of lizards called monitors. (Incidentally, the lizard is called the dragon lizard, too!)

All monitors have long bodies and darting tongues. The Komodo monitor eats other animals, dead or alive. Its sharp teeth and claws make it a very ferocious hunter. It searches among the trees and rocks for an unsuspecting deer or wild pig and attacks on sight.

With its sharp claws, the Komodo monitor digs a secure burrow under the ground. Here, it sleeps through the cool night. If the weather is too hot during the day, it may stay in its burrow to keep cool. The temperature would have to be very hot, however, because the enormous Komodo dragon prefers to keep its body temperature at least 90 degrees!

Can you find and color 15 mistakes?

Chameleon

The chameleon is a lizard that changes color, but not to match its background, as most people think. The chameleon's mood, the amount of light around it and the temperature all affect its color changes. For instance, when it is excited, the chameleon may turn a bright color, even spotty. When it is sleeping, it may turn a very light color. When threatened or cold, the chameleon may turn a dark color.

There are many different species of chameleons. Many have very unusual "decorations." Some have three long horns on their heads. Some have "armor" shaped like a helmet or a hood. Most chameleons have a tail that can grasp onto tree branches and that curls when the lizard is not using it.

A chameleon has a very long, sticky tongue that is sometimes as long as its body! When a tasty-looking insect comes near, the chameleon's long tongue darts out to catch it. It's easy for the chameleon to spot the insect, because each of its eyes can move by itself—so the chameleon can look in two different directions at the same time! These unusual eyes also help the chameleon to see its enemies. When it spots one, the lizard pumps its body up to make it look too big for its enemy to swallow. To avoid being attacked, sometimes the chameleon just drops itself to the ground and disappears among the leaves!

Can you find and color 14 mistakes?

Gila Monster

The Gila (HEE-luh) monster is the only venomous lizard found in the United States. It lives in the desert and woodland areas of Arizona, Utah, California and Mexico, often close to a source of water or damp soil.

A Gila monster is dangerous, but only when it is threatened or attacked. If threatened, it will first gape its mouth wide open to scare the attacker away. If that doesn't work, the lizard will bite the predator and hang on like a bulldog. The venom secreted from glands in its jaws can cause paralysis, even death. The Gila monster uses its venom primarily to subdue and digest food. It tracks food by using its tongue to both taste and smell the food, as many lizards do. Favorite foods of the Gila monster are rodents, carrion (the flesh of dead animals) and bird eggs.

The Gila monster has a big head and thick tail and grows to about two feet long. In fact, everything about this lizard is large, except for its four short legs. The stubby little legs make this desert creature a very slow-moving lizard.

Colorful markings and patterns cover the Gila monster's heavy body. Its black and pink scales look like beautiful Indian beadwork. Perhaps Indians got some of their creative ideas from the Gila monster's beautiful decorations.

Can you find and color 13 mistakes?

<u>Skink</u>

Even though their names are almost the same, the skink is not related to the skunk! Skinks are lizards that can be found in most every part of the world, except Antarctica. Most are small—from 4 to 10 inches long—and half of their length is their tail. Their short legs are not very strong. Flat, shiny, overlapping scales make skinks look polished or glossy.

There are many different species of skinks. Most live in damp, wooded areas. They burrow under leaves, rocks, twigs and rotting wood to hide from their enemies or find insects to eat. The sand skink of North Africa, as you might guess, burrows under sand. In fact, when threatened, this lizard can disappear into the sand in a matter of seconds!

Some skinks can be identified by the stripes on their backs. The five-lined skink lives in the eastern part of the United States. Its dark brown body has five long, beige stripes that turn to light blue at the tail. One western skink species has a shiny, light-brown body with four lighter stripes down its back. You can probably guess its nickname: the four-lined skink!

Can you find and color 12 mistakes?

Painted Turtle

Can you answer this riddle: What reptile grows its skeleton on the outside of its body? Answer: The turtle—because its shell, or carapace, makes up most of its skeleton.

There are many different species of turtles. Some kinds live in freshwater ponds, some live in the sea and some live in the desert. Pond turtles live in the shallow water of streams, ditches and ponds. Their webbed feet paddle them through the water in search of food. Of all the pond turtles, the painted turtle is definitely the prettiest. This 6- to 10-inch-long turtle has bright red, yellow or orange patterns on its legs and on the margins of its shell. These markings even appear on the underside of the shell, or plastron. Painted turtles have different patterns and colors in different parts of North America, but these water creatures are always colorful.

Most turtles have one thing in common: a hard shell. The inside of the shell is made of bone. The outside is made of hornlike scales. Turtles pull their legs, head and tail inside their shell for safety and protection. Once inside the shell, they cannot move.

Can you find and color 13 mistakes?

Diamondback Terrapin

The diamondback terrapin is named for the pattern of raised diamond shapes on its dark shell. (Can you guess what "terrapin" means? It's a word used to describe turtles that are edible.) The diamondback terrapin likes water that is partly fresh and partly salty, and that is why it can be found in bays, marshes and inlets where salty oceans and freshwater rivers mix together. The diamondback used to be found along much of the Atlantic and Gulf coasts, but because of hunting, their numbers have sharply decreased.

The diamondback terrapin spends much of its time in the water, searching for food. Webbing between its toes makes it a good swimmer. But its stubby legs and claws also enable this turtle to walk on land.

Like most reptiles, all turtles, including the diamondback terrapin, are cold-blooded. This means they are not able to warm their own blood, the way humans do. So their temperature is always near the temperature of the air or water where they live. When it is cold, many reptiles hibernate, or sleep for a long period of time. The diamondback terrapin hibernates in the mud all winter long. Can you imagine having a winter home made of mud?

Can you find and color 14 mistakes?

Desert Tortoise

Turtles that live on land are called tortoises. The desert tortoise has found an interesting way of adapting to the very hot and very cold temperatures of the desert: it tunnels deep into the sandy ground. There it is protected from the extremes of heat and cold and from predators, too.

Digging with their feet, desert tortoises dig different tunnels, or dens, for winter and summer. For the cool winter, several tortoises build a large den. With perhaps 30 feet of halls, the den is big enough for 10 tortoises or more. In fact, snakes and rodents sometimes share the large den with the tortoises. The tortoises hibernate in the den all winter.

During the long, hot summer, desert tortoises dig single tunnels that slant about three or four feet into the ground. Here they can keep cool during the hottest parts of the summer. The tortoises come out of their dens very seldomly during the year, usually in spring and fall, when the weather is not too cold or hot. When they do come out to feed, they eat low-growing desert wildflowers and grasses.

Can you find and color 14 mistakes?

Leatherback Turtle

The biggest turtle of all is a sea turtle called the leatherback. Sometimes this turtle can weigh over 1,500 pounds! Its shell, or carapace, can measure up to eight feet long, and overall, from head to tail, the turtle can be 10 feet long. That's the size of a small car!

You can probably guess what the leatherback looks like by its name. Its carapace and underside (plastron) look and feel like thick, dark leather. Its legs are modified into flippers for swimming. The flippers make the leatherback very fast in the water but very slow on land. Leatherbacks eat mainly jellyfish, but sometimes they confuse plastic bags with the jellyfish. Unfortunately, when a leatherback eats a plastic bag, the bag blocks its intestines and kills the turtle.

Because of its size, the leatherback turtle is more comfortable in the water than out of it. In fact, males spend all of their time there. Female leatherbacks, however, do come ashore, but for only one reason: to lay their eggs. Like other female sea turtles, leatherback females come ashore only at night during the nesting season. Because of their great weight and their flippers, they drag themselves along the beach very slowly. Just imagine the sight of hundreds of giant turtles coming ashore at the same time!

Can you find and color 13 mistakes?

Snapping Turtle

The common snapping turtle has a reputation for being very grouchy. It's called the *snapping* turtle because it snaps at an enemy with its powerful, sharp-edged jaws. When it is angry or frightened, the snapping turtle also gives off a very unpleasant odor.

It's easy to recognize a snapping turtle by its large head and the saw-toothed crest along its long tail. These turtles can be found near freshwater rivers or swamps in parts of eastern Canada and the United States, throughout Central America and in parts of Ecuador. They probably don't feel as comfortable when they're on land, because that is when they're most defensive.

The snapping turtle usually eats fish. Much of the time, the turtle sits perfectly still in the water, looking like a clump of mud. When an unsuspecting fish or frog swims by, the snapping turtle darts its long neck out and grabs it. This turtle will go after almost *anything* that swims. In fact, human swimmers have had their toes bitten by snapping turtles!

Can you find and color 15 mistakes?

Matamata

Most people who have seen the matamata turtle agree about one thing: It's bizarre! The matamata has a 12-inch shell that looks like it's covered with irregular ridges and bumps. Algae actually grow all over this strange shell. The matamata has a funny-shaped snout at the front of its triangular-shaped head and loose skin with bits of flesh covering its neck. Its wide neck is about half as long as its shell. When the matamata opens its mouth, it opens it *very* wide.

Believe it or not, the matamata puts that droopy skin, algae-covered shell, long neck, strange snout and wide mouth to good use. Most of the time it sits near the bottom of slow-moving streams of the Amazon rain forest. It breathes by keeping its long snout above the surface of the water, or, if necessary, it can hold its breath for up to 40 minutes. Under the water, the matamata's loose skin waves around with the flow of the water. The bits of flesh may feel the vibrations in the water that swimming fish make, or they may serve to lure fish to come near. Whatever the case, when a fish comes close to the matamata, zap! The turtle's long neck juts out, its mouth opens wide and water rushes in, carrying the fish. The turtle spews out the water and is left with a mouthful of fish.

Can you find and color 15 mistakes?

Tuatara

Over 200 million years ago, even before the dinosaurs, there lived a lizardlike creature called the tuatara (too-uh-TAR-uh). Amazingly, although the dinosaurs died out, the tuataras didn't. Today, you can find these animals only on a few tiny islands off the coast of New Zealand. The tuatara isn't exactly a lizard, a crocodilian or a snake, or quite like any other reptile. In fact, there is no animal living today that is like the tuatara.

Many years ago, tuataras grew to be six feet long. Today, they grow to about two feet long. Their small, rounded bodies are yellowish or olive-brown, and a row of white-tipped, spikelike scales stretches down their backs.

The tuatara lives in a burrowed hole in the ground. Often it shares a burrow with a bird called the petrel. The petrel sleeps during the night and leaves the burrow during the day. The tuatara sleeps in the burrow during the day and comes out at night to hunt for beetles and crickets to eat. It sometimes even eats the petrel!

For many years, tuataras were in danger of becoming extinct. That means they almost all died. Now there are laws to protect them. If people obey the laws, this reptile, with its 200-million-year-old family history, will continue to live.

Can you find and color 13 mistakes?

Answers

Page 3

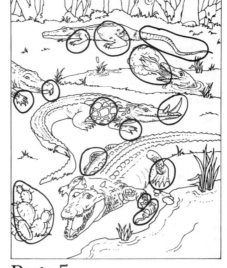

Page 5

Page 7

Page 9

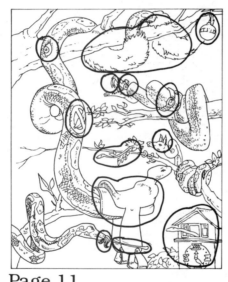

Page 11

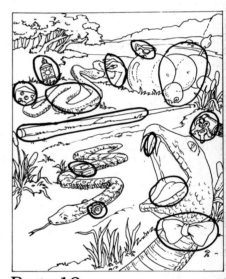

Page 13

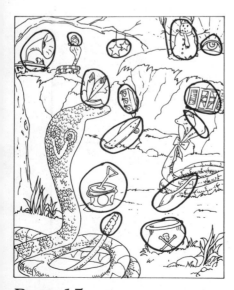

Page 15

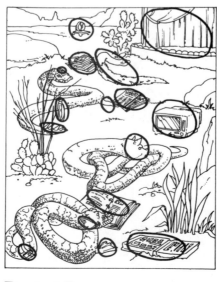

Page 17

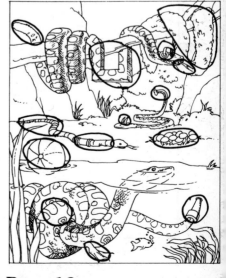

Page 19

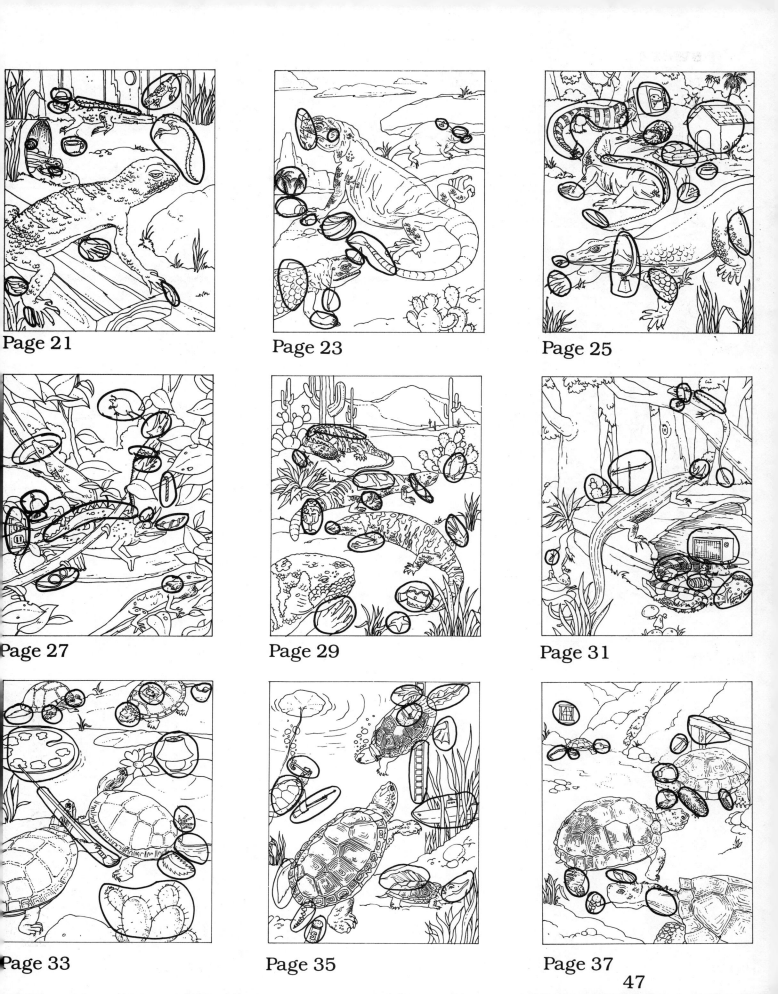

Page 21

Page 23

Page 25

Page 27

Page 29

Page 31

Page 33

Page 35

Page 37

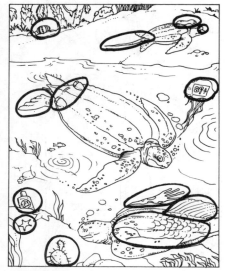

Page 39

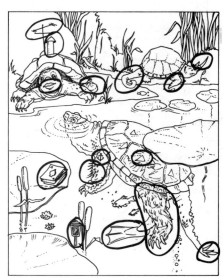

Page 41

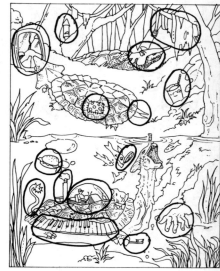

Page 43

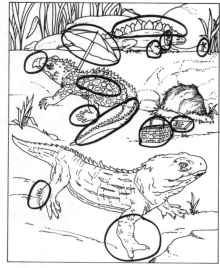

Page 45